The Mystery of the Runaway Scarecrow

THREE COUSINS DETECTIVE CLUB®

00C

The Mystery of the Runaway Scarecrow

Elspeth Campbell Murphy
Illustrated by Joe Nordstrom

BETHANY HOUSE PUBLISHERS
MINNEAPOLIS, MINNESOTA 55438

The Mystery of the Runaway Scarecrow
Copyright © 1999
Elspeth Campbell Murphy

Cover and story illustrations by Joe Nordstrom
Cover design by the Lookout Design Group, Inc.

THREE COUSINS DETECTIVE CLUB® and TCDC® are
registered trademarks of Elspeth Campbell Murphy.

Scripture quotation is from the Bible in Today's English Version
(*Good News Bible*). Copyright © American Bible Society 1966,
1971, 1976, 1992.

Published by Bethany House Publishers
A Ministry of Bethany Fellowship International
11400 Hampshire Avenue South
Bloomington, Minnesota 55438
www.bethanyhouse.com

Printed in the United States of America by
Bethany Press International, Bloomington, Minnesota 55438

Library of Congress Cataloging-in-Publication Data

Murphy, Elspeth Campbell.
    The mystery of the runaway scarecrow / by Elspeth Campbell
Murphy.
        p.   cm. — (Three Cousins Detective Club ; 26)
        Summary: When Buster the scarecrow, a popular feature of the
Fairfield Fall Festival, disappears shortly before the beginning of the
big event, the three cousins set out to find him.
        ISBN 0–7642–2134–5 (pbk.)
        [1. Scarecrows—Fiction. 2. Lost and found possessions—
Fiction. 3. Cousins—Fiction. 4. Mystery and detective stories.]
I. Title. II. Series: Murphy, Elspeth Campbell. Three Cousins
Detective Club ; 26.
PZ7.M95316 Myfc   1999   99–6565
[Fic]—dc21   CIP

ELSPETH CAMPBELL MURPHY has been a familiar name in Christian publishing for over twenty years, with more than one hundred books to her credit and sales approaching six million worldwide. She is the author of the bestselling series *David and I Talk to God* and *The Kids From Apple Street Church,* as well as the 1990 Gold Medallion winner *Do You See Me, God?,* and two books of prayer meditations for teachers, *Chalkdust* and *Recess.* A graduate of Trinity College and Moody Bible Institute, Elspeth and her husband, Mike, make their home in Chicago, where she writes full time.

Contents

"The land has produced its harvest; God, our God, has blessed us."
Psalm 67:6

1

Missing: One Scarecrow

Sarah-Jane Cooper sighed and shook her head sadly. "I miss Buster! I hope he's having a good time on his vacation and everything. But it does seem like an odd time for him to be gone."

She took a bite of toast and chewed thoughtfully, staring off into space.

"Who's Buster?" mumbled Sarah-Jane's visiting cousin Titus McKay. (Titus was never at his best first thing in the morning.)

Sarah-Jane's other cousin Timothy Dawson said, "The only Buster I ever heard of is that scarecrow outside the big restaurant in town."

Sarah-Jane nodded. "That's the one. My mom made him, remember? He was a gift for the restaurant owner, Mr. Wesley. Every year on Labor Day, Mr. Wesley gets Buster out to stand in front of the restaurant. Buster stays there all the way to Thanksgiving. But of course, *this* is really Buster's most important time. October, I mean. After all, he's kind of like the mascot for the whole Fairfield Fall Festival. He rides on a float and everything. So that's why it seems strange that he would just take off like that. And that he hasn't come back yet."

Timothy and Titus paused with cereal spoons halfway to their mouths and stared at her. Sarah-Jane was forever coming up with odd remarks first thing in the morning.

She had seen that look before. It meant: Our Cousin Has Lost Her Mind.

"What?" she asked.

"S-J," said Timothy carefully. "Buster is a scarecrow."

Sarah-Jane gave a puzzled frown. "Right. I just said that, didn't I?"

"But you also said that he took off on vacation or something," said Titus.

"Right," said Sarah-Jane. "He ran away last month by the light of the harvest moon. Doesn't that sound pretty? By the light of the harvest moon? Like a poem or something."

Sarah-Jane read a lot of poems. She also

read books, stories, newspapers, even cereal boxes. If it had words, Sarah-Jane read it.

She was also known in the family for her vivid imagination.

So she wasn't surprised when Titus squeaked, "Ran away? A *scarecrow*?! S-J, where do you come up with this stuff?"

Sarah-Jane sighed. "I did not 'come up with' anything, thank you very much."

Timothy said, "Then where did you get all that about Buster going on vacation?"

Sarah-Jane sighed again and rolled her eyes. It was so hard to get through to some people.

"Where do you think I got it? Buster left a note."

2

A Mysterious Note

"*T*he scarecrow left a note," repeated Timothy.

"That's what I'm saying," said Sarah-Jane.

"How do you know it was from the scarecrow?" asked Titus. "Was it in his own handwriting or something?"

Sarah-Jane groaned. "Handwriting?! Be serious! How's a scarecrow going to hold a pencil? He's a *scarecrow*, for crying out loud."

"I think that's what we've been trying to tell *you*, S-J," said Timothy.

But Sarah-Jane wasn't listening. She drummed her fingers on the table and said thoughtfully, "The note was written on a computer. . . ."

"A *computer*?" said Timothy and Titus together. "You're saying the scarecrow used a computer?"

Sarah-Jane looked at them as if *they* were out of their minds.

"Nooooo," she said super clearly. "I'm saying the note was written on a computer by someone who made it *sound* as if it came from the scarecrow. Scarecrows can't use computers. They're scarecrows."

Timothy and Titus glanced at each other. Now that they knew this wasn't just some wild story Sarah-Jane was making up, it sounded like an interesting mystery.

The cousins loved mysteries, and they were good at solving them. They even had a detective club.

"Why would someone use a computer?" mused Sarah-Jane. "Just because it looks neater? Or because that person didn't want to use his own handwriting? I wonder . . ."

"*S-J!*" cried Timothy. He sounded as if he was about to scream. "Why don't you just start at the beginning and tell us what happened."

"That's what I've been trying to do!" exclaimed Sarah-Jane. "But you two keep interrupting me with all these silly questions."

She took a deep breath and started over. "OK. Mr. Wesley has a scarecrow my mother

made named Buster, who always stands outside the restaurant in the autumn. But last
month—by the light of the harvest moon—
Buster left to go on vacation."

She held up her hand as her cousins
opened their mouths to protest.

"Yes, yes, we all know that scarecrows can't
just run off by themselves." Sarah-Jane paused
and said more to herself than the boys, "Al-
though . . . it does make a good story. . . ."

"*S-J!*" they wailed.

"OK, OK," said Sarah-Jane. "One day last
month, Mr. Wesley came to the restaurant the
same as usual, expecting to see Buster the
same as usual. But Buster wasn't there. Just a
note taped to the door."

"What did the note say exactly?" asked
Titus.

"I happen to know exactly," said Sarah-
Jane, "because Mr. Wesley gave me a copy of
it."

She went to the sideboard, opened a
drawer, and pulled out a sheet of paper. It was
a photocopy of a short note that had been
typed on a computer.

Timothy and Titus crowded round to read
it.

Dear Mr. Wesley and Good People of Fairfield,
    Much as I love standing here day after day, I have a yearning to see the world. So I'm off—by the light of the harvest moon—on a much-needed vacation. I will be back when you figure out where I've gone. Keep looking up!

                Your Scarecrow,
                Buster

"Strange!" murmured Titus. "Very, very strange!"

"Wait," said Sarah-Jane. "It gets stranger."

3

Peculiar Photographs

"What could be stranger than a scarecrow going on vacation?" asked Timothy.

"How about a scarecrow sending back pictures of himself on vacation?" suggested Sarah-Jane.

Timothy and Titus stared at her.

"You have *got* to be kidding," they said.

"Nope!" said Sarah-Jane. "I have the photographs right here."

She pulled an envelope out of the drawer and spread the pictures out on the sideboard.

"Where did you get these?" Timothy asked in amazement.

"Mr. Wesley gave them to me," said Sarah-Jane. "A couple of days after Buster left, Mr. Wesley got a photograph in the mail. And every couple of days after that he'd get more.

"He hung up the note and the pictures outside his restaurant. People got really interested in them. But no one could figure out where Buster was. Then a few days ago, the pictures just stopped coming."

"Weird!" declared Titus.

Sarah-Jane said, "Mr. Wesley marked them on the back in the order they arrived. So it's OK to mix them up if you want to. Jill says the mystery about Buster has gotten people more excited about the Fall Festival. But everybody's worried that he won't get back in time." (Jill was the mayor of Fairfield and a friend of Sarah-Jane's family.)

"Why did Mr. Wesley give the pictures to you?" asked Timothy.

Sarah-Jane said, "He knew you guys were coming for the Fall Festival. And he knows we have a detective club. So he said maybe we could figure out what's going on and find Buster in time for the parade."

"No pressure there," said Titus.

Sarah-Jane and Timothy laughed.

"But seriously, though," continued Titus. "Do you think there's a clue in the photographs?"

Sarah-Jane shrugged. "Who knows? I've been over them a dozen times already, but I

can't make heads or tails of them." (This was a phrase Sarah-Jane had picked up from her reading, and she kept trying to work it into conversations.)

The photographs showed the scarecrow doing ordinary vacation-y things: standing outside a motel, going into a gift shop, stopping at a gas station—and so on.

Titus said, "These pictures could have been taken anywhere. I mean, there's no clue—like mountains or the ocean—to tell you where he went on his vacation."

Sarah-Jane said, "And even if you *could* figure out where Buster went, the pictures don't tell you where he is now."

Timothy frowned. "The photographs aren't very good, either." (Timothy knew this because he was very good at photography himself.) He said, "They're off-center. Like this one. It shows more of the sign in the background than it does of the scarecrow."

"Here's one where you see only a little bit of the sign," said Sarah-Jane.

"That's what I mean," said Timothy. "Why have him standing in front of a sign at all if you can't even tell what it says? Just a couple of letters are showing. It seems that whoever took the pictures could have come up with more interesting-looking backgrounds."

Titus said slowly, "Maybe interesting backgrounds would have given too much away. Do you know what I mean? The note said Buster would come back when people had figured out where he'd gone. But maybe it's like a game. Maybe whoever took the pictures didn't want to make it too easy for people to guess where Buster was."

Sarah-Jane nodded. What Titus said made sense to her.

Timothy nodded, too. But Sarah-Jane could tell that he was just itching to take the pictures over again and get them right. All the cockeyed signs in the background were bothering him.

"Anyway," said Sarah-Jane. "The photographs have stopped coming. The parade is tomorrow. Buster isn't back yet. And nobody has figured out where he is. What are we going to do about it?"

4

Another Mystery

*T*he truth was, they didn't have the slightest idea what to do about it.

Titus said, "It seems that there must be a clue in these pictures. Otherwise, why send them? Just as a joke?"

Sarah-Jane said, "Maybe it was a joke to take Buster in the first place. A pretty dumb joke if you ask me. But it seems that whoever took him *wants* him to be found."

"Then why doesn't he just send another note from Buster, telling where he is?" asked Timothy grumpily.

Sarah-Jane understood how Timothy felt. Sure, it was exciting and interesting to come across a mystery. But what the cousins really liked about mysteries was *solving* them. An un-solved mystery was enough to make any detective feel a little grumpy. And Sarah-Jane wasn't feeling very hopeful about solving this one.

The detective cousins shuffled through the pictures some more, hoping something would jump out at them. But nothing did.

Titus had a sudden thought. "What about the postmarks on the envelopes? Wouldn't that tell you where Buster was when he mailed the pictures? I mean—if a scarecrow *could* mail anything, that is."

"Good question, Ti," said Sarah-Jane. "The ZIP codes were all from places around here. Wherever the scarecrow went, he didn't go too far away."

The cousins were quiet for a while, just thinking things over.

They simply had no idea how to answer the questions that kept swirling around in their heads:

Where had Buster gone?

Who had taken him?

Why?

And most important, where was Buster *now*?

It was pretty discouraging!

"So, S-J," said Timothy. "Do you have any *other* mysteries around here that need solving?"

"As a matter of fact, I do," said Sarah-Jane. "But if we can't find a scarecrow, I doubt if we can find a rare coin."

Timothy and Titus glanced at each other. Were they about to hear one of Sarah-Jane's wild Our-Cousin-Has-Lost-Her-Mind stories?

Sarah-Jane guessed what they were thinking. And just for that, she didn't say anything at all.

"*S-J!*" wailed Timothy and Titus together.

"What?" asked Sarah-Jane calmly.

Titus sighed. "You can't just say something like that and then not tell us what it's about."

"Why not?" asked Sarah-Jane.

"Aurrggh!" said Timothy.

"OK, OK," said Sarah-Jane. She put on her best storyteller's voice. "It all began one dark and stormy night in September."

5

A Strange Tale

"*R*eally?" asked Timothy, fascinated. "A dark and stormy night?"

Sarah-Jane cleared her throat. "Um . . . well, maybe not. I mean, it *could* have been a dark and stormy night. It certainly sounds better for the story. But who knows?"

"S-J . . ." began Titus.

"OK, OK," said Sarah-Jane quickly. "I don't know if it was a dark and stormy night. All I know is that a rare coin from Mr. Clark's collection *mysteriously vanished.*"

"Vanished?" asked Titus. "You mean it was stolen?"

Sarah-Jane said in her best Mysterious Voice, "Who can tell? It was just here one day and gone tomorrow." (This was another phrase Sarah Jane liked that she had picked up from her reading.)

"Who's Mr. Clark?" asked Titus.

"He's just a nice man with a coin collection," said Sarah-Jane.

It didn't sound so mysterious when she put it like that.

"When did this happen?" asked Timothy.

Sarah-Jane shrugged. "It could have been anytime, I guess. Mr. Clark doesn't get out the coins all the time. So he can't say for sure when the coin disappeared.

"He doesn't even have that big of a collection. He just has a few really nice ones that he keeps in a display box on a bookshelf. One day recently he noticed that his best coin was gone."

"Mysteriously vanished," said Titus.

"Exactly!" said Sarah-Jane.

"Just one coin?" asked Timothy. "If someone was going to steal one coin, why not take the whole collection?"

Sarah-Jane frowned. "I wondered about that, too. Nothing else was taken. No sign of a break-in or anything."

"Hmm," said Titus. "Sounds like an inside job to me."

"Well, there's just Mr. and Mrs. Clark,"

said Sarah-Jane. "But they often have company over for dinner. Friends. Business people. Anybody could have taken it. A person could just say he had to go to the bathroom or something. It would be easy enough to slip into the study on the way back and take the coin."

"Nice," said Timothy. "You invite people for dinner, and somebody steals from your coin collection."

"Well," said Sarah-Jane. "The Clarks aren't *absolutely positive* that's what happened. So of course, they didn't want to go around accusing people."

Titus said, "I suppose the coin *could* have fallen out of the box the last time Mr. Clark was looking at them. Maybe he just didn't notice it was missing until later. Is that possible?"

"It's *possible*," said Sarah-Jane.

"But not likely," said Titus.

"No," agreed Sarah-Jane. "Not likely. They looked everywhere, of course. I even helped them. But no coin."

Timothy and Titus nodded.

The cousins were very good at finding things. Especially Sarah-Jane. If she hadn't found the coin, it probably wasn't there.

Timothy suddenly thought of something.

"Who else besides Mr. Clark is a coin collector? Wouldn't that person be the chief suspect?"

"Yes," said Sarah-Jane. "Except Mr. Clark doesn't know anybody else who collects coins."

6

The T.C.D.C.

"*T*oo many questions!" exclaimed Timothy. "Not enough answers."

"*No* answers, you mean," said Titus.

"Tell me about it," sighed Sarah-Jane.

She didn't want to admit it, but she was beginning to doubt if she was such a good detective after all.

Sarah-Jane didn't give up very easily.

But she had already given up on finding Mr. Clark's lost coin.

And she was just about to give up on finding the runaway scarecrow.

So she was not in the best of moods when the doorbell rang.

She was in an even worse mood when she saw who was standing on her front porch.

Billy Michaels.

Again.

He was an older boy who lived nearby.

And he was always giving her a hard time about one thing or another.

Lately he had been teasing her mercilessly about Buster the Scarecrow.

"What do you want?" asked Sarah-Jane crossly.

Billy grinned at her. "So, Cooper," he said. "I just stopped by to see if you've found the scarecrow yet."

"No," said Sarah-Jane. "Go away and stop asking me that."

"The parade's tomorrow," Billy reminded her.

"I am perfectly well aware of that," said Sarah-Jane in her best Teacher Voice. If she could have, she would have sent Billy Michaels to the principal's office right that minute.

Billy peeked around her.

"Who are those two guys?" he asked.

Sarah-Jane sighed and rolled her eyes. She had a pretty good idea that Billy already knew who "those two guys" were. He was just trying to annoy her.

And it was working.

Big time.

"Not that it's any of your business," she said crisply. "But these are my cousins Timothy Dawson and Titus McKay."

"Are they detectives, too?" asked Billy innocently.

"As a matter of fact they are," replied Sarah-Jane. "For your information, we are the T.C.D.C."

"What's a 'teesy-deesy'?" asked Billy, sounding genuinely puzzled.

"It's letters," explained Titus. "Capital T. Capital C. Capital D. Capital C. It stands for the Three Cousins Detective Club."

"No kidding?" asked Billy, surprised.

"No kidding," said Timothy.

"So—you really think you might find the scarecrow after all?" asked Billy.

"If it's the last thing we do," said Sarah-Jane.

7

Funny Weird

Sarah-Jane didn't exactly slam the door. But she did shut it rather firmly.

Then she and her cousins peeked out the window to see if Billy was gone.

He hung around on the porch for a few minutes as if he was thinking of ringing the doorbell again. Then he turned and shuffled away with his hands shoved in his pockets, his shoulders slumped.

"That's funny," said Titus.

"Funny ha-ha? Or funny weird?" asked Timothy.

"Funny weird," said Titus.

"What's funny weird?" asked Sarah-Jane.

"Billy Michaels," said Titus.

"You can say that again!" exclaimed Sarah-Jane.

"No, I'm serious," said Titus. "There's something strange going on here."

"Tell me about it!" muttered Sarah-Jane. Then she saw that Titus really was serious. "What do you mean, strange?" she asked.

"It's the way Billy keeps asking you about the scarecrow," said Titus. "I don't think he's just doing that to tease you. I think he really wants to know where the scarecrow is. I think he really, *really* wants to know."

Sarah-Jane thought about this for a minute. When someone really annoys you, you figure that's why he acts the way he does—just to annoy you. It's hard to realize he might have any other reason for acting the way he does. Billy didn't annoy Timothy and Titus the way he did her. So maybe they could see something going on here that she couldn't. It was possible, anyway. But that still left a big question:

"What does Billy Michaels care where Buster is?" she asked.

Titus shrugged. "I don't know. I just think there's something funny weird going on."

"And I'll tell you something else funny weird," said Timothy. "I know Billy Michaels acts like a total goof. But underneath I think he's scared."

"Scared!" exclaimed Sarah-Jane. "Billy? Of what?"

"I don't know," said Timothy. "It's a feeling I picked up just now."

"Me, too," said Titus. "Now that you mention it."

Sarah-Jane didn't say anything. Her brain was too busy wondering: *What does Billy Michaels have to be scared of?*

8

The Prankster

*T*itus said, "You know, I could be wrong about Billy really wanting to know where the scarecrow is. Maybe Billy already knows where Buster is, because *Billy* is the one who took Buster in the first place.

"Maybe now Billy realizes that taking the Fall Festival mascot was a dumb thing to do. So maybe he wants to put it back in time for the parade. Before he gets in trouble."

"Then why doesn't he just put it back?" asked Timothy. "Why does he keep bugging S-J about finding Buster?"

Titus shrugged. It was a good question. "Maybe he's afraid of getting caught in the act of putting Buster back," he suggested. "Maybe he thinks no one will suspect him if Sarah-Jane finds the scarecrow."

Sarah-Jane shook her head. "No, I think you were right the first time, Ti. I don't think Billy knows where Buster is. I don't think Billy is the one who took him. Sure. I can picture Billy playing a dumb joke. But I can't picture Billy writing that note. Can you?"

The three detective cousins went to the sideboard to look at the note again.

"See what I mean?" asked Sarah-Jane. "It says *'good people of Fairfield.'* And *'yearning to see the world.'* And *'by the light of the harvest moon.'* Does that sound like *Billy* to you?"

Timothy and Titus had to admit that it didn't.

"It sounds more like an English teacher wrote it," said Timothy.

"My point exactly," said Sarah-Jane. "It sounds like the work of . . . of . . . a clever prankster."

Sarah-Jane liked the sound of the word *prankster*. It sounded more interesting than someone who just played dumb jokes.

She was just putting the note away when she knocked over the stack of photographs. They fell all over the floor.

Sarah-Jane bent down to pick them up. Timothy and Titus helped her.

"That's funny," said Sarah-Jane suddenly.

"Funny ha-ha? Or funny weird?" asked Titus.

"Funny interesting!" said Sarah-Jane. "Look!"

9

The Puzzle

Sarah-Jane plopped down on the floor and began lining up her photographs of Buster. Timothy and Titus watched her in amazement.

"See?" cried Sarah-Jane.

Timothy and Titus looked.

"See what?" asked Timothy. "It's just three not-very-good pictures of the scarecrow on vacation."

"Right," said Titus. "The first one shows the scarecrow standing in front of a building. But you can't tell what it is. In the next one he's by a billboard of some kind. And in the third one he looks like he might be at a train station. There's a sign with the number 2. Does that mean Track 2?"

"That's what I mean!" cried Sarah-Jane.

"Don't look at the scarecrow. Don't look at where he is. Look at the *signs behind him*."

"But the signs don't say anything," said Timothy.

"Yes, they *do!*" exclaimed Sarah-Jane. (After all, she was the one who automatically read everything she could get her hands on.) "Yes, they do! Not by themselves, of course. You have to put them together. I didn't notice it until I dropped the pictures and they sort of fell together in a way that made sense."

She pointed to the first photograph. There was only a little bit of the sign showing. Just two letters.

"*I. F*" said Timothy. "*If!*"

"Right," said Sarah-Jane. "The word *if*. That could be the beginning of a sentence maybe. Or maybe it comes in the middle of a sentence. I'm not sure. But I think it's the beginning, because look at the next picture."

This one showed the scarecrow in front of a sign that had two words showing: *you want*.

Then came the picture at the train station with the number 2.

"See what I mean?" asked Sarah-Jane. "If you put these three pictures in order, it spells out '*if you want to . . .*' "

"That's why the pictures are so off-center!"

exclaimed Timothy. "Whoever took the photographs had to get in the words he needed for the puzzle."

"Right!" cried Titus. "So it doesn't matter what the scarecrow is doing in the pictures. It doesn't even matter what order the pictures came in. All that matters is putting the signs in order so you get the message. I mean, that's what we're saying, aren't we? That the signs spell out a message?"

"Sure seems like it," said Sarah-Jane, scrambling for more photographs. " *'If you want to . . .'* If you want to what? Find the scarecrow, of course."

10

The Message

*I*t was sort of like putting together a jigsaw puzzle except that the "pieces" were words.

The cousins were so excited it was hard to keep from bouncing up and down and scattering the photographs every which way.

But they knew they had to calm down and get organized.

Sarah-Jane had already lined up three pictures. And there were just a few more. So they set these other pictures over to the side. In no particular order. Where they could *all* see them.

At least with a jigsaw puzzle, you had the picture on the box to follow. But here, you didn't even know what the puzzle was until you solved it.

Titus found a picture where the sign in the

background said *"find the."*

Timothy found a picture that didn't have any sign at all—just a close-up of the scarecrow.

The boys put these pictures after Sarah-Jane's.

And sure enough, it was just as she had predicted. The message said, *"If you want 2 find the [scarecrow] . . ."*

At the same moment, all three cousins pounced on a sign that said simply *"Look!"*

It made sense to put it next.

Only three more pictures to go.

The cousins closed their eyes and each picked one.

Sarah-Jane's had only two little words: *"in the."* But it made sense to put them after *"Look!"*

So now the message said, *"If you want 2 find the [scarecrow] Look! in the . . ."*

Quickly Timothy and Titus laid down their photographs.

But there were no more words.

Timothy's picture showed the scarecrow standing in front of a billboard. You couldn't tell what it was advertising, but the art showed a row of big black birds.

"Neat-O art," muttered Timothy. "But

what does it mean? What are those? Crows? Makes sense, I guess, if you've got a scarecrow."

He put the picture in the line.

Titus's photograph had no sign in the background at all. It just showed the scarecrow standing next to a tree. Some of the leaves had fallen, and you could clearly see a little nest in the tree.

Titus very nicely let Sarah-Jane put the last photograph in place. After all, Buster was sort of hers since her mother had made him. And the photographs were sort of hers since Mr. Wesley had lent them to her.

Then the Three Cousins Detective Club sat back and read the message on the floor:

"If you want 2 find the [scarecrow] Look! in the [crows] [nest]."

11

The Crow's Nest

No one said anything right away.

It was a strange feeling to be so satisfied and so disappointed all at the same time.

Sarah-Jane had been right about a secret message in the photographs. A puzzle that told where the scarecrow was. And they had solved the puzzle. Great! That was very satisfying.

But what did it *mean*?

They knew where the scarecrow was. But they *didn't* know where he was. Actually, they had no *idea* where he was. And that was very disappointing.

"A *crow's nest*?" asked Timothy. "Do crows even live in nests? I suppose they must. I never thought about it before."

"I think they do," said Titus, who was interested in all kinds of animals. "I think they build them out of sticks on the tops of tall trees. Or even telephone poles. I've even heard of people having crows for pets. I wonder how they do that. . . . And I've heard crows like shiny things. I wonder why that is. . . ."

Timothy shrugged. He was used to Titus wondering out loud about animals. "We're kind of getting off the point here, Ti. The puzzle said the scarecrow was in the crow's nest. OK. So say crows build their nests in tall trees or telephone poles. Does that sound like the kind of place you'd hide a scarecrow? I mean, wouldn't someone have *noticed*?"

Titus couldn't help laughing. He agreed that of all the places to hide a scarecrow, a crow's nest was about the craziest.

Sarah-Jane was only half listening to all of this. She had picked up the dictionary and looked up *crow*. It didn't tell her anything helpful, nothing she didn't already know, that is. And it didn't say anything about where crows build their nests.

But that didn't matter. The fact was, Sarah-Jane simply loved dictionaries. Sometimes she looked through them just for fun. The only problem was, if she ever *had* to look up a word, it could take her forever. That was because she kept getting distracted by all the other words.

For example, she had just wanted to look up *crow*. But the dictionary told her that there was a Native American tribe called *Crow*. That was interesting. She hadn't known that. And the dictionary said that the little lines grown-ups got at the outside corners of their eyes were called *crow's-feet*. She was sure she had heard her mother talk about that. And the dictionary said that there was something called a . . .

Sarah-Jane let out a shriek that caused her

cousins to jump about a foot in the air.

Timothy clapped his hand over his chest. "S-J! Don't *do* that!" he said.

"How many times do we have to tell you?" gasped Titus.

"It's here!" Sarah-Jane cried. "It's right here in the dictionary!"

"What's there?" asked Timothy and Titus cautiously. They were not nearly as crazy about dictionaries as Sarah-Jane was. And they couldn't imagine what had gotten her so excited. They weren't even sure they wanted to know.

Sarah-Jane saw That Look again. "No, I have not lost my mind," she said. "It's right here in the dictionary. *Crow's nest!* And guess what! It has nothing to do with crows!"

12

The Hiding Place

"*A* crow's nest is not a crow's nest?" asked Titus. "What kind of sense does that make?"

"Actually, it makes a lot of sense when you stop to think about it," said Sarah-Jane—more to herself than to the boys. "It's a cute way of putting it, really, because of the way crows build their nests up high. . . ."

"S-J," said Timothy, trying to stay calm. "What's a crow's nest?"

"Oh! Sorry!" said Sarah-Jane. "I guess I got a little sidetracked there. The dictionary says a crow's nest is that little round platform at the top of a ship's mast. What's the mast? Isn't that the tall pole that holds up the sails? Anyway, the sailors can climb up there and use the crow's nest as a lookout."

"*That's* what the secret message means?"

asked Titus. "That the scarecrow is hiding on a ship's mast? That doesn't make any more sense than if he was hiding in a real crow's nest in a tree."

"No, it doesn't, does it?" agreed Sarah-Jane. "But the dictionary says *crow's nest* can be *any* high place that's used as a lookout."

The cousins thought about this for a minute.

"That doesn't narrow it down very much, though," said Timothy.

"It does if Buster is back in Fairfield," said Sarah-Jane. "Fairfield doesn't have very many high places."

Titus gave a little gasp. "The note!" he exclaimed. "The note said, *'Keep looking up!'* That was a clue, and we didn't even know it! I thought *'Keep looking up'* was just a nice thing people say. I thought it meant 'Keep having faith in God.'"

"I think that's what it *does* mean," said Timothy.

"Right," said Titus. "And maybe that's what the person who wrote the note meant. But what if he *also* meant it as a clue?"

"So you're saying he meant it *literally*," murmured Sarah-Jane. "He meant *really* keep

49

looking up. And then what? We'll find Buster's hiding place?"

"Could be," said Titus. "It certainly fits with the idea of the crow's nest."

"Well, here's a question for you," said Timothy. "What are we waiting for?"

13

The Search

*W*henever Timothy, Titus, and Sarah-Jane visited one another, they liked to bring their bikes along. You never knew when a bike would come in handy.

And this was one of those times.

The cousins were allowed to ride all over Fairfield as long as they wore their helmets and stayed together and got home on time. They had to tell Sarah-Jane's parents they were going out. But it was OK if the cousins didn't know exactly where they were going.

And this was certainly one of those times!

Sarah-Jane's father was out at work, and her mother was in the office-workroom upstairs. Sarah-Jane's mother had a small sewing and decorating business. She was on the phone with a client when the cousins tiptoed in.

Sarah-Jane acted out putting on her helmet and climbing on her bike. It meant, *We're going out riding, OK?*

(She was glad she didn't have to act out that they were going to look for a scarecrow in a crow's nest. That could have taken a while.)

Her mother nodded and acted out eating. It meant, *Be home in time for lunch*.

So the detective cousins hurried downstairs, grabbed their bikes, and went off on the search.

"Where do we start?" asked Timothy.

"Good question," said Sarah-Jane. "Let's just start riding and figure it out as we go along."

Fairfield was an old town with a lot of beautiful old houses. Many of the houses were well over a hundred years old. The style of building back then had been fancy, fancy, fancy. So a lot of the houses in Fairfield had little towers and turrets and high attic windows.

Also, most of the houses were painted luscious colors. People came from all over to see them—especially during the Fairfield Fall Festival.

So three kids riding slowly by looking up at the houses was not that unusual. No one

would know what they were really looking for.

"Hmm," said Titus. "A lot of these houses have what you could call crow's nests, I guess. But we can't exactly knock on the front door and say, "Excuse me. That's a nice-looking tower room you have there. Do you happen to have a scarecrow hiding in it?"

Timothy and Sarah-Jane agreed that this wouldn't be the best approach. But they had no idea what the best approach would be.

Soon they were in the center of town. Here a lot of the old houses had been converted into "quaint little shops." It was very busy today, with lots of people buying things like candles and fudge.

Tomorrow would be the kickoff of the Fall Festival with the big parade.

But with no Buster.

Unless they did something.

Fast.

Sarah-Jane looked at the visitors, who were oohing and ahhing at the pretty buildings.

It was a funny thing about living in a place. Sometimes you didn't really notice the things you saw every day. Sometimes visitors noticed more about a place than the people who lived there.

Sarah-Jane looked around and pretended to be a visitor.

The first thing that caught her eye was a big red brick building across the street at the end of the block. It stood back from the street on a small hill. With the high tower in the middle, it was easily the tallest building in town. It was the Fairfield courthouse. Sarah-Jane had lived in Fairfield all her life, but she had never been inside.

"There," she said.

Timothy and Titus looked where she was pointing.

"Can we even go in there?" asked Timothy doubtfully.

"I don't know," said Sarah-Jane.

"Well, at least we can take a closer look," said Titus.

So they went to take a closer look. They walked their bikes up the long sidewalk to the building.

They tilted their heads back and looked up at the tower.

If any place in Fairfield could be called a crow's nest, this would be it.

And it turned out they were right about that.

Because from the highest tower window, Buster smiled back at them.

14

Buster

"*B*uster!" squeaked Sarah-Jane. "It's really Buster!"

Sometimes it's hard to believe it when something you've only guessed about turns out to be true.

"What do we do now?" asked Titus. "Go in there and tell somebody?"

They all turned to look at the wide steps and the huge front door.

"Yes," said Sarah-Jane. "We have to go in there and tell somebody. You guys go. I'll wait here with the bikes."

"Hey, not so fast, S-J," said Timothy. "This is your town, remember."

"That's right, ma'am," drawled Titus. "We're just strangers in these here parts."

Sarah-Jane sighed. "Oh, all right. I'll go.

But one of you guys has to come with me. The other one can stay here with the bikes."

Timothy and Titus looked at each other.

"Oh, all right," said Titus. "S-J and I will go. Tim can wait with the bikes. If we're not back in five minutes, call in the cavalry."

Sarah-Jane bravely led the way. She had come this far looking for Buster. No reason to chicken out now that she had found him. After all, Buster did sort of "belong" to her.

She took a deep breath, marched up the steps, and pulled on the door.

Nothing.

The door was locked.

Of course it was. It was the weekend. But now what did they do?

"Now what do we do?" Timothy asked when Sarah-Jane and Titus joined him at the foot of the steps.

The cousins backed up so they could look up at the tower and see Buster in the window.

So near and yet so far.

"Do you know anyone who would have the key?" asked Titus. He sounded as if he didn't think she would but that it didn't hurt to ask.

Sarah-Jane started to say no. But then she thought about it for a minute. And it was as if a little bulb went on in her head. Really.

"Jill," she said.

"Jill!" cried Timothy and Titus together.

Of course! The mayor would have the key to the courthouse. Or she would be able to get it.

Without another word, the cousins hopped on their bikes and rode as fast as they could to Jill's house.

They knew where she lived because they had once solved a mystery there.

Jill answered the door even before they could ring the bell. It was as if she was expecting them.

"Jill! Jill! We found Buster!" gasped Sarah-Jane.

"You'll never guess where he is!" exclaimed Timothy.

"There was a secret message in the photographs that sort of said where the scarecrow would be," said Titus, all in a rush. "But we still had to hunt for him."

"Hey, great work, you guys!" said Jill. "Just let me grab my jacket and the keys to the courthouse, and I'll be right with you."

The cousins looked at one another.

They hadn't said anything about the courthouse.

So how did Jill know where Buster would be?

15

Buster's Pocket

"*W*hat?" asked Jill when she came back to find the cousins staring at her.

"It was you!" cried Sarah-Jane. She tried to sound shocked, but she couldn't help laughing. "You took Buster on vacation. You left the note. You sent the photographs. You put him in the tower. You're the prankster!"

Jill laughed, too. "I was hoping somebody would figure it out! I should have known it would be you three."

The cousins left their bikes at Jill's house and walked back to the courthouse with her.

"Why?" asked Titus. "Why did you do all that?"

"To drum up excitement for the Fall Festival," said Jill. "I guess you could call it a publicity stunt."

"It worked!" said Sarah-Jane.

"Yes," said Jill. "Everyone seemed very interested in the note and the photographs. But no one guessed where Buster was."

"He was on vacation," said Sarah-Jane.

"Not really," said Jill. "I took the photographs all in one day. I just mailed them at different times. Buster's been up in the tower window, looking down on Fairfield ever since he left the restaurant."

"And nobody noticed?" asked Timothy.

"Nobody noticed," said Jill.

"And not even Mr. Wesley knew where Buster was," said Sarah-Jane.

Jill laughed. "Pete Wesley and my husband, Jack, have been playing practical jokes on each other ever since they were in college together. Pete figured Jack had something to do with Buster's disappearance. But Jack didn't know anything about it at all. Neither of them guessed it was me. After all, I'm the *mayor*. But finally I fessed up.

"I'm glad to say Mr. Wesley thought it was a pretty good joke. It was even good for business at his restaurant. But time was running out on solving the puzzle. So I told Mr. Wesley to give the photographs to you. I figured if anyone could solve the mystery, it was the T.C.D.C."

"But what if we *hadn't* been able to solve it?" asked Timothy.

"Well," said Jill. "Buster would have shown up in time for the parade. But it wouldn't have been as much fun. And no one would have won the prize."

"There's a prize?" asked the cousins.

"Oh, yes," said Jill. "Free passes to the Fairfield Inn Restaurant. And the puzzle solvers get to ride on the float with Buster."

"Neat-O!" said Timothy.

"EX-cellent!" said Titus.

"So cool," said Sarah-Jane. Then she added, "Billy Michaels will be glad to know Buster has been found. He's been very upset about it."

Jill looked at her in surprise. "Why would Billy be upset about Buster?"

Sarah-Jane shrugged. "Beats me."

They had reached the courthouse. Going up the steps to the big door was not the least bit scary with the mayor along.

And it was exciting—not scary—to go up the winding stairs to the tower. The little room at the top was just used for storage. But there was a wonderful view of Fairfield.

And best of all, there was Buster.

Sarah-Jane couldn't resist giving him a big hug. As she did, he tipped over a little.

Something fell out of his pocket and rolled onto the floor.

An old coin.

They all just stood there staring at it for a moment.

"Hmmm," said Jill thoughtfully. "Something tells me Billy Michaels has some explaining to do."

The cousins weren't there for Billy's explanation. But they heard about it later.

Another kid had said he would pay Billy to steal the coin from Mr. Clark's collection when Billy and his parents were at the Clarks' for dinner. The kid said he would leave the money in the scarecrow's pocket and Billy was supposed to pick up the money and leave the coin. Well, Billy picked up his money and left the coin. But before the other kid could get the coin, Jill had come along and taken the whole scarecrow.

The other kid was furious and demanded his money back. Billy gave it to him. By that time Billy realized what a bad thing he had done and just wanted to get the coin back so he could get it back to Mr. Clark. But he had no idea where the scarecrow was or what would happen to the coin.

"Not one of the smartest schemes I've ever heard of," said Timothy.

"You can say that again," said Titus. They had just had the most *fabulous* dinner at the Fairfield Inn. The grown-ups were still inside talking. But the cousins had been excused to come out and sit on the porch with Buster.

"Did you have a good time at the parade today, Buster?" Sarah-Jane asked him.

"*S-J!*" said Timothy and Titus together.

"What?"

"He's a scarecrow."

"Of course he is," said Sarah-Jane. "But that doesn't mean he can't have fun, does it?"

Timothy and Titus opened their mouths to reply . . . and closed them again.

Sometimes it just didn't pay to argue with Sarah-Jane.

The End